# Detective Small
## in THE AMAZING BANANA CAPER

## Wong Herbert Yee

HOUGHTON MIFFLIN COMPANY
BOSTON 2007

For fans of Fireman Small
— W.H.Y.

The text of this book is set in Berliner Grotesk.
The illustrations are in charcoal pencil and watercolor.

*Library of Congress Cataloging-in-Publication Data*

Yee, Wong Herbert.

Detective Small in the amazing banana caper / written and illustrated by

Wong Herbert Yee.

p. cm.

Summary: When shop owners call on Detective Small to track down a banana thief, he
follows the clues to a likely suspect, then learns that the real culprit is still on the loose.

ISBN-13: 978-0-618-47285-7 (hardcover)

ISBN-10: 0-618-47285-1 (hardcover)

[1. Detectives—Fiction. 2. Robbers and outlaws—Fiction. 3. Animals—Fiction. 4. Stories
in rhyme.] I. Title.

PZ8.3.Y42Det 2007

[E]—dc22
2006009821

Manufactured in China

SCP 10 9 8 7 6 5 4 3 2 1

In the middle of town, where buildings stand tall,
You will find the office of Detective Small.
A crack private eye with a nose for crime,
Detective Small gets his man *every* time!

Late last night, while the city was sleeping,
From market to market, a shadow came creeping.
The crook tiptoed past, pulled a mask on his face—
The *perfect* crime was about to take place!

When the stores opened the very next day,
Owners stood gaping in shock and dismay!
Horrified grocers discovered the theft—
Busted-up crates were all that was left!

From Chinatown to Little Havana,
Uptown, downtown—not ONE banana!

The markets offered a healthy reward.
Psychics were summoned; no tip was ignored.

Police were baffled; they could not pretend.
The trail had gone cold, every lead a dead end.
Somebody, somewhere, had to make the call
To ask for the help of *Detective Small!*

Good thing our gumshoe was free at the time!
Small rushed at once to the scene of the crime.

He combed the market in search of some clue,
Found hairs and a print: *was it from the thief's shoe?*

In dumpsters, down alleys, Small picked up the trail.
It stopped where a scrap of cloth snagged on a nail.

Back in his office up on the ninth floor,
Detective Small bolted the locks on the door.
He kicked off his boots, wiggled his toes,
Pulled out a hanky to wipe his nose.

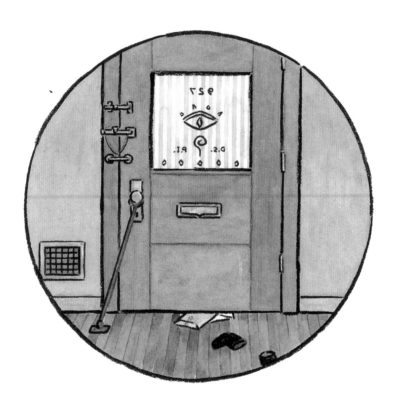

After taking a ten-minute snooze,
Small was ready to sift through the clues.

The hairs were not from a cat or a dog;
The print was too big for a cow or hog;
The cloth dyed yellow was some type of tweed . . .
WHO could've pulled such a dastardly deed?

*Why* bananas? Why not kumquat, or grape?
*"Great gumshoe!"* cried Small. "Could it be an APE?"

Detective Small made a sketch of the crook.
He circled names in the telephone book.

Dressed head to toe in a nifty disguise,
He went to find out his suspect's shoe size.

From junkyard to warehouse, in fancy hotels,
Small sniffed about for banana-type smells.

Ice cream entrepreneur Folsom Fox
Said there was an ape snooping out by the docks.
Before he left to check on that gorilla,
Our gumshoe ordered a scoop of vanilla.

Small spotted the subject—was hot on his heel.
He nearly nabbed him, but slipped on a peel!

The chase continued across railroad tracks,

High atop buildings,
in boarded-up shacks.

A trail of bananas led straight to the ape.

The monkey surrendered, no chance of escape.

Back in his office up on the ninth floor,
Detective Small bolted the locks on the door.
He kicked off his boots, wiggled his toes,
Pulled out a hanky to wipe his nose.
Small clicked on the TV to watch the news,
As he flipped through his notebook of clues.

Nothing turned up when cops searched the ape's boat;
No holes were found in his pants or suit coat.
*"Great gumshoe!"* cried Small.
"These boot prints don't match!"
Detective Small still had a burglar to catch!

The following day on his way to lunch,
Small ducked into the costume shop on a hunch.

Yikes! An ape suit rented just three days before
Was never returned to the Halloween store.

*Meanwhile* . . . outside, there's quite a commotion.
It's Folsom Fox's new sundae promotion!

That clue was the last to bust open the case.
It all added up; things fell right into place.
Detective Small elbowed his way past the mob.
This gumshoe was ready to finish the job!

He fought through a flurry of cones and cream puffs.
Small tackled the culprit and slapped on the cuffs.

In a storeroom he recovered the loot,
Along with the missing gorilla suit!

The innocent ape Folsom Fox tried to frame
Thanked the detective for clearing his name.

Back in his office, up on the ninth floor,
Detective Small bolted the locks on the door.
He kicked off his boots, wiggled his toes,
Pulled out a hanky to wipe his nose.

The mystery's been solved; now Small can relax.
It's easy-peasy, when you have ALL the facts!